A GRACEFUL ESCAPE

A shot film screenplay

Akhilesh Verma a.k.a RageSider

Gravity Realm Entertainment

CONTENTS

Title Page	1
INT. LITTLE ROOM - MORNING	5
INT. MAIN HALL - MORNING	6
EXT. YARD - MORNING	8
INT. LITTLE ROOM - DAY	10
EXT. YARD - DAY	11
EXT. ROAD - DAY	13
EXT. PARK - CONTINUOUS	14
INT. HALL - DAY	15
INT. LITTLE ROOM - EVENING	17
INT. LITTLE ROOM - MORNING	19
INT. HALL - MORNING	21
INT. LITTLE ROOM - MORNING	23
INT. LITTLE ROOM - DAY	25
EXT. YARD - DAY	27
INT. LITTLE ROOM - DAY	29
EXT. YARD - DAY	31
EXT. ROAD - DAY	33

INT. LITTLE ROOM - MORNING

The old things are scattered on the red mat. The sketch pens and some papers are also there. The incomplete sketches are plotted on some papers.

Walls are filled with toon sketch, Colorful toons. Sketches of the mickey mouse and the babies.

A rough bed. The old quilt on the bed. A boy, PINKU, 14 years old, in the quilt. He is facing the wall, watching the toons. Living in that world. He seems without any worry.

A LOUD SOUND OF DAYA

                    DAYA (O.S.)
          Where is my breakfast?

No reply from Pinku.

The sound becomes more louder.

                    DAYA (O.S.) (CONT'D)
          Pinku!

He tries to get up in lazy mood.

                    DAYA (O.S.) (CONT'D)
          Where are you, slacker?

Pinku realizes that Daya is calling him. He throws the quilt, jumps out from the bed.

He wears his broken slippers and runs toward the door.

                                        CUT TO:

INT. MAIN HALL - MORNING

A beautiful carpet, set of sofa and a table are placed on the carpet.

DAYA, middle age, wearing a white pantsuit, is sitting on the sofa. A black shiny stick is stationed near him.

He picks a betel from the table and chews it.

He looks toward the door and stands up quickly. He takes his stick with him.

DAYA
What were you doing, little brat?

Pinku is standing before him. Silently, looking toward the ground.

Daya wafts up his stick.

DAYA (CONT'D)
Are you deaf?

Pinku looks into his eyes. He answers in very low voice.

PINKU
Sleeping.

DAYA
What? Speak louder.

PINKU
I was sleeping, father!

Pinku looks the ground again. Daya goes back to the sofa. He turns to Pinku.

DAYA
You are a real pain in ass! Tell me...
who will do the work?

Silence.

> DAYA (CONT'D)
> What are you waiting for, punk? Go and prepare my breakfast.

Pinku steps forward.

> DAYA (CONT'D)
> Wait, wait... I'll tell Rame kaka to prepare breakfast.

Pinku changes his walk toward his room.

> DAYA (CONT'D)
> Have you washed my car?

He shakes his head in negative.

> PINKU
> No.

Daya throws his stick on sofa. He runs to slap him. But he manages to stop himself.

> DAYA
> You brat! What were you doing last night?... Go and wash my car.

Pinku exits from the front door.

> DAYA (O.S.) (CONT'D)
> Rame, O Rame...! Prepare my breakfast. I'm getting late.

CUT TO:

EXT. YARD - MORNING

A car is parked in the yard. The condition of car is not too dirty. It's looking well.

There are some old clothes, some buckets and washing powder. Pinku is fitting the water-pipe into the tap.

He switches on the tap. Water flows through the pipe.

Bucket is full.

He picks up some clothes, takes a bucket and swifts to the car.

He stops in the midway, turns to the fences. He starts looking the fences.

MOMENT LATER

                    DAYA (O.S.)
          Rame! I'm getting late.

He recognizes that he'll has to wash the car. We wakes up from his dream and continues his job.

As he starts washing, a hand stops him.

                    RAMAN
          What are you doing?

                    PINKU
          Washing the car! What's the matter?

RAMAN, 25, wearing white vest and an old pajama. He is looking like a healthy young man.

                    RAMAN
          I told you many times not to do these
          works. Why are you washing the car?

Pinku drops the bucket down.

PINKU
Father told me.

Raman snatches all the things from Pinku.

RAMAN
Go to your room. I'll take care of this.

Pinku rolls out.

CUT TO:

INT. LITTLE ROOM - DAY

Pinku is sitting on the mat.

He looks his papers and sketches. He picks up the paper and starts completing the unfinished one.

He hears SOUND OF CAR from the yard.

                    DAYA (O.S.)
          Rame! Close the door, I'm leaving.

This sound interrupts his work.

He gets up and peeps out from the window. He sees there is no one for closing the door.

                                        CUT TO:

EXT. YARD - DAY

Pinku is standing at the door. He closes the half door.

He stops and watches the road.

A hand catches Pinku from behind. Pinku feels shocked and turns backward.

It's Raman.

                    RAMAN
          Pinku?

                    PINKU
          Ham... I... I...

He tilts his neck down before Raman.

                    RAMAN
          You were wanting to go outside?

Pinku looks Raman as guilty person.

                    RAMAN (CONT'D)
          Go.

                    PINKU
          What?

                    RAMAN
          Go.

A change occurs on Pinku's face. He hugs Raman.

                    PINKU
          Thanks, Raman uncle.

                    RAMAN
          But come soon, else you'll be in a big
          trouble.

PINKU

Eyes full of tears, tears of joy.

> PINKU
> I want to see behind these walls just
> once, Raman uncle. I'll come soon.

Raman smiles back.

CUT TO:

Pinku is running like a free kite.

He sees flowers on the road-side. He sits near the flowers, he touches them softly.

As he gets up, he sees _ _

EXT. PARK - CONTINUOUS

Children are playing in the park.

Pinku touches the sea-saw. Two girls are playing on sea saw. They are laughing loudly.

Pinku is watching them, living with their happiness.

> BOY (O.S.)
> Hey brother!

Pinku turns to the sound. He sees a boy on the slider, is calling him.

> BOY (CONT'D)
> Wanna slide.

Pinku looks the slider.

> PINKU
> No, thanks.

> BOY
> Come on brother, have some fun.

Pinku joins him.

> PINKU
> But I don't know what to do.

> BOY
> Don't worry I'll show you.

Boy slips on the slider. He slides down very fast. Pinku seems very joyful. Pinku does same as the boy did.

As Pinku reaches at the bottom, he sees _ _

DAYA is standing before him.

> CUT TO:

INT. HALL - DAY

PINKU

In moaning position, eyes full of tears.

> DAYA
> What were you thinking?

> PINKU
> Nothing, father.

Pinku sobs.

> DAYA
> (In anger)
> Nothing... what are you doing in that stupid place?

Daya rises his stick.

> DAYA (CONT'D)
> Tell me first, how did you get out from the house?

No answer from Pinku.

> DAYA (CONT'D)
> Oh... than you are not going to tell anything.

> PINKU
> Father... I... just want to... see...

Daya interrupts.

> DAYA
> What you want to see? Don't you have books? Am I not spending on you?... On your demands?... Everything I pro-

vided you. Am I wrong?

                    PINKU
No, dad.

                    DAYA
Than what? I'm very kind with you...
and you...

Daya steps forward and slaps Pinku. Pinku falls down. Drops of
blood appear on his lips.

                    DAYA (CONT'D)
Stop your tears, you brat! You have
everything in your life, besides that
you betrayed me... You cheated on
me!

Pinku stands up.

                    PINKU
Sorry, father.

                    DAYA
You are immoral boy. No food for
today. This is your punishment.

                    PINKU
Father.

                    DAYA
This is your fault. You saw bad, you'll
reap bad.

                                        CUT TO:

INT. LITTLE ROOM - EVENING

The papers and sketches are scattered on the mat.

Under the table_ _

Pinku is sitting. Keeping his head on his knees. He looks at his papers.

> PINKU
> What is my fault?

Pinku picks a paper, it is a laughing sketch of Mickey mouse.

> PINKU (CONT'D)
> Why are you laughing at me?

He tosses the paper.

Covering his face with his arms, he begins crying. He screams loudly.

> PINKU (CONT'D)
> No... no. Is... only... pain... for me?
> What is my fault?

He hears a knocking sound at door. He does not response.

Raman, waiting at the door.

> RAMAN (O.S.)
> Come on boy, open the door.

Pinku gets up and opens the door.

As Raman enters in the room, he picks Pinku in his arms. He carries him to the bed.

> RAMAN (CONT'D)
> Don't cry, Pinku, everything will be
> all right.

He washes Pinku's blood.

                    RAMAN (CONT'D)
          Don't cry.

Pinku hugs him tightly.

                    RAMAN (CONT'D)
          Take rest, little boy, everything will
          be fine.

He drops Pinku on his bed. He covers him with quilt.

                                        CUT TO:

INT. LITTLE ROOM - MORNING

Pinku, covered with quilt, is sleeping. Reflection of sun ray shines on his face.

He wakes up.

He sees a girl, sitting on the mat, is coloring the pictures. The glass of her watch is reflecting sun light.

> PINKU
> Who are you?

She turns to him.

> MUSKAAN
> Hi, I am Muskaan.

Pinku comes to her. He sees his pictures in her lap.

> PINKU
> Those are mine.

> MUSKAAN
> Sorry.

He snatches the picture from her.

> PINKU
> You are not supposed to take those.
> Those are mine.

A sad look on her face

> MUSKAAN
> How rude!

> PINKU
> What are you waiting for? Get out
> from my room.

> MUSKAAN

Fine.

She makes a careless exit from the room.

INT. HALL - MORNING

Muskaan is sitting on the sofa.

Pinku comes to her. He has his papers.

>PINKU
>Sorry.

She looks his hands with paper.

>MUSKAAN
>I'll forgive you when you will give me
>that drawing.

Pinku sits on the ground. He has some color pens also.

>PINKU
>Come here.

Muskaan joins him. She takes the paper and starts coloring.

>MUSKAAN
>I love filling colors. Did You draw
>those pictures?

>PINKU
>Yes, I like drawing.

>MUSKAAN
>Those are really good.

She continues her work. Pinku is watching her.

>MUSKAAN (CONT'D)
>You didn't tell your name?

>PINKU
>It's Pinku, you... Muskaan, right?

>MUSKAAN
>Right. Do you have more pictures?

> PINKU
> Yes come to my room, I'll show you.

Muskaan, full of cheers.

> MUSKAAN
> O it's Great! Let's go than.

                                        CUT TO:

INT. LITTLE ROOM - MORNING

Pinku hands over an old file to Muskaan. Muskaan opens it. She sees numbers of pictures in the file.

>   MUSKAAN
>   These are really great!

>   PINKU
>   By the way, you didn't tell me what
>   are you doing here?

Muskaan puts the file on table.

>   MUSKAAN
>   My parents are not so rich, but they
>   want to provide me good education.
>   Daya uncle is a social worker. So he
>   said, he will take care of my educa-
>   tion.

Pinku interrupts.

>   PINKU
>   You mean, father?

>   MUSKAAN
>   He is your father?

>   PINKU
>   Yes.

>   MUSKAAN
>   You are lucky. You have a kind father.

Pinku becomes sad. Muskaan catches his intensions.

>   MUSKAAN (CONT'D)
>   What's the matter?

                    PINKU
          Nothing. You just enjoy.

Muskaan smiles back.

                                    FADE TO:

INT. LITTLE ROOM - DAY

Pinku is sitting on the chair. Muskaan is sitting on bed, eyes full of tears.

Pinku turns to her.

> PINKU
> Stop crying now. Learn how to compromise.

Muskaan stands from the bed.

> MUSKAAN
> But I never...

> PINKU
> Muskaan, look I can understand your feelings, but it is worthless to cry.

Pinku comes to her. Both sit on bed. He holds her face in his palms.

> MUSKAAN
> I was thinking, Uncle Daya is very kind. He was ready to take care of my educations... But he has taken my freedom.

She starts crying again.

> PINKU
> No, Muskaan, don't cry.

> MUSKAAN
> You leave me alone.

> PINKU
> What?

> MUSKAAN

Leave me alone, I said.

Pinku holds her hand.

> MUSKAAN (CONT'D)
> What have I done, Muskaan?

She slaps him.

> MUSKAAN (CONT'D)
> Can't you understand? Leave me alone.

> PINKU
> Fine, I am going.

Pinku leaves the room. Muskaan is weeping continuously.

CUT TO:

EXT. YARD - DAY

Near the car, Pinku is sitting. He has a bucket near him. Raman
sees him and comes to him.

> RAMAN
> Pinku. What am I looking? Again?

Pinku does not answer. Raman sits with him.

> RAMAN (CONT'D)
> Tell me what's the matter?

Pinku looks at his face.

> PINKU
> Raman uncle, why we have to serve
> father? Why we have to live like a
> slave in our own home?

A sudden change appears on Raman's expressions. He tries to control his emotions.

> RAMAN
> You are taking care of Muskaan. You
> are very nice boy.

> PINKU
> Don't try to change the topic, uncle.

Raman offers his lap to sit. Pinku accepts it.

> RAMAN
> Reality is that... we are slaves, we all
> are in this house... slaves.

> PINKU
> But how? He is my father and your
> brother.

> RAMAN
> No. He is not. The truth is...

> PINKU
> What? Tell me the truth, please.

Raman takes a long breath.

> RAMAN
> Than listen, Daya Nath Shastri works as social worker. He adopts the children of poor family. He promises them to give better life... but after adopting them, he uses them.

> PINKU
> He is not my father! I am also... like Muskaan...

> RAMAN
> We all share the same fate, boy.

> PINKU
> What about you?

> RAMAN
> We have the same story. Like you, Daya's father adopted me.

Raman tries to control his tears again. Pinku tries to consoles him.

> PINKU
> Uncle, I have decided. I have suffered, but I will not let Muskaan suffer. I will not.

CUT TO:

INT. LITTLE ROOM - DAY

Muskaan is still weeping. Pinku enters.

> PINKU
> Muskaan, Do you know where is your home?

> MUSKAAN
> Yes, but why?

Pinku holds her hands.

> PINKU
> Because we are escaping from this house, from our fear, from our prison. I have suffered in this house, but I will not let you.

Muskaan hugs him.

> MUSKAAN
> Are you saying truth? You will take me to my home?

> PINKU
> Yes, Muskaan.

> MUSKAAN
> You wait, I am going to take some goodies.

Pinku stops her.

> PINKU
> No, no... I don't want any memory of this place with me.

> MUSKAAN
> As you wish, Pinku.

AKHILESH VERMA

She hugs again.

EXT. YARD - DAY

Pinku and Muskaan, holding hands, are running toward the gate.

They stop.

They see Daya is standing between them and gate.

> DAYA
> Where are you both going?

Both scares a little.

> DAYA (CONT'D)
> You brats!

> PINKU
> No more dirty words, old man.

Daya never excepts this answer.

> DAYA
> You punk! How dare you to talk like
> this?

> PINKU
> And how dare you to talk like this?

> DAYA
> Show some respect, I'm your father.

> PINKU
> Father? I know who you are. You are
> nothing but a dirty person who gam-
> bles with the innocent life.

Daya is about to slap Pinku.

> MUSKAAN
> Stop old man, you can't do this.

> DAYA

You want to know what can I do?

Pinku and Muskaan hold hand of each other tightly.

                    PINKU
          Let's go.

Daya blocks their way.

                    DAYA
          You can't leave without my permis-
          sion.

                    PINKU
          You are not my God, No, No more. No
          more suffer, No more fear...
                    (to Muskaan)
          Come on Muskaan.

They both run. Daya tries to stop them. But He slips on the grass.

                    DAYA
          Come back... came back.

They both cross the gate.

                                        CUT TO:

EXT. ROAD - DAY

Pinku and Muskaan, both are running on the road. Forwarding their steps toward a new future.

                    NARRATOR (V.O.)
          No one knows what happened next!
          But this is sure Pinku had gain success.
          Success of being fearless. And the per-
          son who wins against fear gets his am-
          bition for sure...

                    FADE TO BLACK

                    THE END.

9 798621 826062